THE THIN BLUE LINE

WHERE JUSTICE BORDERS MORALITY

By

C. M. Russell

authorHOUSE™

1663 LIBERTY DRIVE, SUITE 200
BLOOMINGTON, INDIANA 47403
(800) 839-8640
WWW.AUTHORHOUSE.COM

First published by AuthorHouse 02/10/05

ISBN: 1-4208-1849-X (sc)

Printed in the United States of America
Bloomington, Indiana

This book is printed on acid-free paper.

For Milicent De'Ance Lavizzo-Russell.
You have been my inspiration. Thank you. I love you.

INTRODUCTION

When justice fails, and crime prevails, who is at the frontline? Sworn to protect and serve, these men and women in blue must abide by rules while confronting criminals who have no rules. These men and women are counted upon to toe the line between justice and morality. This is their story; the story of two young veteran Chicago Police Officers and their trials and attempts to apprehend a violent, murderous criminal. Officer James Robinson, the elder of the two by one year, along with Officer Cliff Young, are highly respected throughout the department. The Westside district these officers are assigned to patrol has gained a reputation for its violence and is amongst the busiest areas in the city. Assigned to patrol this area, these Westside officers have been partners for over seven years, since they came out the training academy together.

TABLE OF CONTENTS

CHAPTER ONE: Friday Night

Preparing For Roll Call

In the locker room, James is meticulously checking his equipment and making the proper adjustments as needed as he gets dressed for Roll Call. Joking with several of the newer, less experienced officers, he begins to tell a story about Officer Xavier and the auto-thieves.

…"So we're driving down the alley and we hear Xavier screaming on the radio for help. 'He's running Northbound in the alley approaching Douglas Blvd' …. well, we were in that same alley and we see them running right towards us. Poor Xavier is out of breath and still running full speed, so me and Cliff bail out the squad and give chase with him. The offender sees us coming and turns to run into one of the back yards with Xavier still truckin' right behind him. The next thing I remember hearing is ZZZZIIIIIPP, TWANNNNNNG…….ZZZZIIIIIIIPP, TWANNNNNG, and seeing both the auto thief and Xavier on their backs knocked out and a clothesline still vibrating!!!!"

As all the rookies and Officer Xavier laugh, in comes Cliff.

"Wassup fellas!"

Cliff greets his coworkers as he walks to his locker and begins getting dressed. The mood is very upbeat amongst the crew as they laugh and joke around in a family atmosphere. Final preparations are made as they lace up their boots, check their ammo and weapons, put on their vests, and lastly fasten their gun-belts to their waists. James, Cliff, Xavier and the younger officers are now ready for roll call.

Once in the Roll Call room, all the officers pair off and sit down still laughing and snickering about Xavier's clothesline incident. In the moments waiting for their commanding officer to enter the room and begin their tour of duty, Cliff notices one of the rookies has forgotten to affix his star to his uniform, and signals to remind him. The younger officer hurries to affix his star as the commanding officer enters the room.

"Good Morning, it is really busy out there tonight so I am gonna' keep it short and sweet" the Westside Command Lieutenant states.

"There is still the same old shooting and killing and drug dealing at the same spots…typical for a Westside Friday night, so just be careful and back up each other."

The Lt. then takes attendance.

"11…Officers Ricks and Collins, 12…. Officers Kelley and Barnes, 13…Officers Baker and Xavier, and 14… Officers Robinson and Young. That's all, so be careful… Dismissed"

The team of officers then proceeds out the Roll Call room to their squad cars and begin driving off to their respective assignments.

"J, that has got to be the shortest roll call ever" Cliff states.

"Yeah it must be busy out there tonight; it's a full moon out too!! Yeah, it's gonna' be one of those nights" James replies as he cuts his radio on.

"You feel like driving tonight? I only got a few hours sleep?" James asks.

"No problem. Let's roll!"

"Westside 13, ... EMERGENCY!!....Man With a Gun"

No sooner than Cliff and James cut on their radios, they hear the heavy volume of radio traffic being transmitted.

"Lynda is dispatching tonight so we are in good hands." Cliff says as he listens to the radio.

"Good, because she is our lifeline.   You ever notice how a good dispatcher can get you the help you need when you need it. It is like she can hear it in our voices. We need her to stay on the radio." James replies assuredly.

"Westside 13"….. "Westside 13"….the dispatcher calls.

Officer Xavier's voice can be heard answering, "Westside 13, go ahead" as he awaits his assignment.

"Westside 13, there is a loud party at 2013 South Pulaski, and the neighbor wants you to ask them to cut the music down. Do you copy?"

"Westside 13, 10-4."

Officers Baker and Xavier then proceed to their assignment. While en-route to their assignment Officer Xavier notices an individual in the alley who immediately turns away as their squad car passes by.

"Stop the car!" Officer Xavier yells as he opens the squad car door and begins to unholster his weapon.

"What'd you see?" Officer Baker asks as he stops the car.

"That guy back there in the alley, he just tucked a gun in his waistband" replied Officer Xavier.

Suddenly the unmistakable sound of gunshots rings out…. BOOM, BOOM, BOOM…BOOM, BOOM, the back windshield of their squad car then shatters out.

"EMERGENCY" Officer Xavier yells into the radio as he and his partner dive behind the squad car for cover.

Officer Baker then begins yelling "Westside 13, Westside 13, EMERGENCY"

Lynda, the dispatcher, recognizes the urgency in their voices and orders all other units to stay off of the radio and then answers Officers Baker and Xavier.

"Westside 13 you have the air."

"Westside 13, EMERGENCY!!.... Man with a gun ...." The radio clicks.

"Westside 13, we are being shot at. My partner is in foot pursuit ...20th and Trumbull" the radio clicks.

Understanding their pleas for assistance, Lynda is heard on the radio dispatching all units available throughout the city "CODE 3, CODE 3, there is a CODE 3 at 20th and Trumbull, any units available please respond."

Lynda then calls out to Westside 13 for any updates, or descriptions.

"Westside 13."

"Westside 13" Xavier answers as he can be heard over the radio running and breathing heavily.

" He's a male, black, about 23 years old, black hooded sweatshirt, blue jeans, just ducked between the houses in the gangway!!!" The radio then goes quiet.

"...BOOM"

"Baker, take that side and cut your radio down so you don't give yourself away," Xavier whispers as he does the same.

For the two officers are now engaged in a deadly game of hide and seek, after having lost sight of the offender in the gangway. Slowly, the two officers scan the area and inch deeper into the dark gangway.

"Baker, he is definitely close. You can still smell the gunpowder" Xavier states.

"What was that noise? X, there was a noise over there" Officer Baker whispers to Xavier.

Quietly, they both listen. Then they both hear it again, more faint than before but they hear it none the less.

Officer Baker whispers to Officer Xavier "you cover the gangway, I'll check right there" as he inches closer to the shadow covered doorway. An empty soda can moves, and Officer Baker shines his flashlight in that direction in a startled fashion.

"A rat" he sighs, with his heart pounding in nervous anticipation.

Meanwhile, Officers Cliff Young and James Robinson are the first to arrive at 20th and Trumbull and see the bullet-riddled squad car. Weapons drawn, they approach with caution from the rear on both sides of the tattered squad car looking for the officers.

"Clear...They are not in there!" Cliff tells James.

James then calls over the radio for their location "Westside 14."

"Westside 14, we are on scene at 20th and Trumbull where are the officers?"

Lynda calls out again for Officers Xavier and Baker "Westside 13, you have Westside 14 on scene where are you?"

Xavier replies over the radio "We are in the gangway at approximately BOOM!!!"

Then radio silence. Stunned from hearing the gunshot just two doors away, James and Cliff both run in that direction fully expecting to see Xavier and Baker standing over the body of the man that just shot at them in the squad car moments earlier. All responding units, along with the dispatcher heard the gunshot over the air as Officer Xavier was talking.

Officer Baker begins yelling "CODE 3, EMERGENCY CODE 3!!! OFFICER DOWN, GET ME SOME HELP OVER HERE!!! ROLL ME AN AMBULANCE, CODE 3"

Things get very confusing and hectic over the radio as numerous units begin cutting one-another out trying to ascertain the officers' location, and offender info.

"2008 South Trumbull, 2008 South Trumbull. Send the Ambulance to this location Code 3!" Cliff responds seeing the officers in the gangway.

"Which way did he go?" Cliff asks Officer Baker as he holds his motionless fallen partner.

Baker points in the direction from which they had originally entered.

"Is he ok?" James asks, already knowing the answer, but hoping for a different one.

Officer Baker's head drops. The empty feeling one gets in their heart and chest, a feeling of shock and disbelief, a feeling of anger and despair sets in on the three officers as they watch their friend, their partner, their coworker, take his final breath.

"....I Lost Him...."

Out of the corner of James' eye he sees movement in the backyard just on the other side of the alley and begins to cautiously proceed to investigate with his partner Cliff at his side. Slowly they exit the gangway and cross the alley to gain a tactical position on the person on the other side of the fence that is now with his back turned and crouched down by the side of a house.

"Freeze, Don't Move." James orders.

"Show me your hands, and slowly walk backwards, towards the sound of my voice."

Slowly, the offender shows compliance by raising his empty hands high above his head but does not move towards the officers. Suddenly he bolts towards the front of the house and then down the street. Officers Young and Robinson give chase by hopping the rear fence into the yard and running after the subject. Hard to understand over the radio because of the heavy radio traffic, Lynda attempts to get them the help they need as they radio in the directions.

"Westside 14, we are northbound on Spaulding approaching 20th street... Male, Black, 20's, black hooded sweatshirt and blue jeans.... Westbound through the yards approaching Christiana.... in the alley now.... on Christiana...Northbound on Christiana.Westbound through the yards.......I lost him in the yards between Christiana and Homan"

"Cliff what's your location and where did you last see him?" the dispatcher asks.

"Westside 14, my partner and I are at 1737 South Homan in the yards. Subject last seen in this vicinity" James responds to the radio.

The radio, still buzzing with activity clicks. "Westside Command to dispatch."

Lynda responds, "Go ahead Westside Command."

The Roll Call Lieutenant asks, "What is the status of the officer."

"Ambulance 26 is on scene and confirms D.O.A." the dispatcher regretfully responds.

Suddenly all the radio chatter and clicking stops... ..Radio silence. Now more than ever there is a sense of urgency to apprehend this vicious killer. Officers Young and Robinson are a full 4 blocks from the original crime scene and literally within yards of the offender.

"James, don't move."

"If we were right behind him and he can suddenly disappear like that, he is close. Really close."

Cliff cautiously whispers as they now begin to use hand signals to communicate, listening for the slightest noise. At least 40 officers converge on the area. With the massive influx of officers, residents begin to come outside to watch unknowing of the danger that they were in.

"Cliff" James calls out pointing his attention to a black hooded sweatshirt balled up and thrown in the corner of the fences.

"He's changed clothes…'Westside 14," James calls over the radio.

"Westside 14, go ahead."

"Westside 14, let all the responding units know that the offender has removed his black-hooded sweatshirt and is now wearing an unknown colored shirt and blue jeans. Call out the dogs to try and get a scent and have the responding units set up a perimeter" James orders.

"The dogs are already on scene at 20th and Trumbull and are starting to retrace the offender's steps. Just stand by at your location until the dogs have worked their way to you," the dispatcher explains.

No sooner does the dispatcher finish talking does the radio click again.

"Canine 27." The responding dog handler calls to dispatch and has picked up a scent.

"Canine 27, I am in the rear yard across the alley from the shooting, the dog has located the murder weapon tucked alongside the house. We need the weapon processed for prints."

Meanwhile, the offender has blended in with the numerous citizens whom have come outside to watch all the commotion and police activity. The offender slowly slips away into the mass of people which has gathered after hearing of the shooting. Officers spend the next several hours doing an exhaustive search from yard-to-yard and house-to-house.

Several hours have passed since the shooting and death of Officer Xavier, and Officers Young and Robinson have just finished being debriefed by the Homicide Detective Board. By now the news media is covering the breaking story from various spots throughout the city and on every channel.

"I've got to call home," Cliff states to his partner as they leave the debriefing boardroom.

"Yeah, me too! My pager has been blowing up for a few hours now" James responds as they stop at the desk to make their calls.

Cliff starts to dial as water begins to fill the wells of his eyes, fully feeling the effects of the traumatic events of earlier. He hangs up.

"I'll talk to them when I get home," Cliff grievingly states as he walks off.

Meanwhile, James places his phone call as he begins to gather his composure.

"Hey honey, listen, just listen for a minute," he exclaims to his worried and frantic wife.

"This is the first chance that I have had to call, I am o.k, and Cliff is o.k," James continues as his voice begins it break. "I know you have heard what happened, and yes we were involved. I'll explain later. Do me a favor and call Cliff's family to let them know that everything is o.k. I'll be home soon." James immediately hangs up as he too, is now overcome with the death of his coworker and friend.

Meanwhile, Officer Cliff Young is driving home, replaying the events of the night and reminiscing on the times he's had with Officer Xavier. He chuckles as he remembers Xavier at a family picnic. And again, as he remembers Xavier just hours earlier in the locker-room cracking jokes with James. Cliff then begins to remember the aftermath of the shooting. Running up to the gangway, smelling the gunpowder and watching the offender as he stood with his hands in the air. As Cliff has these flash backs, the traffic-light has run a full cycle turning green and back red again as he just sits at the light. Cliff regains his composure and continues his drive home to his family. Once in the drive way, the grieving officer walks up to his waiting family and without saying a word, embraces them.

CHAPTER TWO: Saturday Night

"...Do What You Gotta' Do..."

It has been almost a full day since the shooting and Officer Young is now preparing himself and his equipment for work. Cliff pays special attention to his gear as he begins to make the transition from family-man to officer, and takes on an officer mindset. Each time he puts this uniform and its equipment on, Officer Young is reminded and understands that there is a chance that it may be his last. As he checks his appearance in the mirror one last time, Officer Young then turns to his wife and kisses her goodnight.

"I love you," he whispers in her sleeping ear and then turns to say goodnight to his daughter.

"I love you too, be careful," is heard as he exits the room.

At the police station, officer morale has diminished. Each officer now contemplates the what-ifs in their minds. In the locker room, the mood is somber as each officer now faces their own mortality and why they chose this profession in the first place.

"Who needs this drama?" one young officer states.

"They want you to have a degree, for what, to get shot at? You don't need a degree for that! I can make the same salary as a banker, an accountant, almost anything, and not get shot at while doing it," he continues.

"Hold On!" James interrupts.

"Is that what you think this is about? A paycheck? A salary? A degree to get the job? Hell, you need a degree to get most jobs now….If you feel like you don't need to be here then maybe you should be an accountant, banker, or something else….like you said, you got the degree!!!" James says in a confrontational manner.

"So what are you trying to say, that Xavier gave his life to the department because he chose not to be an accountant?" James asks.

"Xavier did not GIVE his life to the department, that coward last night TOOK his life…. You ask who needs this drama? You, me, him, him, him, and every other officer who put on the uniform daily knowing full-well that in an instant, anything can happen and we may not be coming home…Now there is a coward out there that I know damn well Xavier wants brought in…Dead or Alive."

James' face is now literally an inch away from the young officer's as they stare each other down. All the officers in the locker room then attempt to get between the two sensing the imminent clash.

"Wassup fellas," Cliff offers the usual greeting, but without the usual flare and upbeat tone, as he enters the locker room unaware of the tension that has arisen between his partner and the younger officer.

"James, will you leave the kid alone and finish gettin' ready?"

James and the young officer then break eye contact and finish prepping for roll call. Noticeably angered by the younger officers' actions, James sits in the roll call room waiting for the tour to begin.

"You know he would've kicked your ass," Cliff whispers to his partner as he takes his seat for roll call.

"He was out of line. You came in at the end of it." James exclaims.

"True. But this is not the time, nor place to check him."

"ATTENTION!!" The Westside Command Lieutenant yells, cutting off Officer Young.

"As many of you know, we lost one of our own last night, under some tragic circumstances.... I'm not one to lecture but I will say this, we are family. We back each other up like family. We celebrate as a family, and we grieve as a family. Yesterday, one of our brothers was killed. His family is our family. Reach out to them, support them, and console them in their time of need. A collection has been started, so give what you can.....Officers, yesterday someone violated our family member in the worst way....Bring Him To ME!"

The Commanding Lieutenant pounds his fist on the podium to emphasize the seriousness of the matter.

"Bring Him To Me. I don't care what it takes, or how you do it...Bring Him To Me!!....There is a cop killer walking free while a family mourns...BRING HIM TO ME!!!!...Dismissed...Officers Young and Robinson, see me after roll call in my office," the Lieutenant orders.

The officers then file out to their respective squad cars and assignments silently, as if they were suddenly focused and on a mission.

As James and Cliff walk into the office after roll call they are told, "Close the door and sit down," the Lt. orders.

"You guys and Officer Baker were the only ones who actually saw this guy. Therefore, you are the strongest link we have to solving the case....Because there is so little to go on, you just tell me what you need in terms of manpower, overtime, and equipment. I am telling you now, 'It's Approved'...."

The commanding Lieutenant then leans across the desk and lowers his tone.

"DO WHAT YOU GOTTA' DO. I'll back you 100 percent. We'll worry about paperwork later, just bring him to me."

The Commanding Lieutenant then sits back in his chair and asks if there were any questions and dismisses the officers.

The officers cut on their radios as they exit their commanding Lieutenant's office and head toward their squad car. Once again the radio traffic is nonstop indicating a busy Saturday night is in store.

"Westside 14," the dispatcher calls.

"Westside 14," James responds looking to his partner stating 'here we go.'

"Westside 14, there are numerous calls coming in of a person shot at Douglas and Trumbull and the Fire Department confirms that there is an ambulance en-route to that same location. I need you to start heading that way to investigate. Do you copy?" Lynda states as she gives the assignment out.

"Westside 14, we copy."

Officers Young and Robinson then activate their emergency equipment and proceed to the crime scene to investigate. Meanwhile, several units have monitored the assignment given to Westside 14 and have proceeded to go to the crime scene. The first officers on-scene are two rookies assigned to unit Westside 11.

"Westside 11," Officer Collins calls out to the dispatcher.

"Westside 11, we are on scene at Douglas and Trumbull. A witness stated that an older Chevy Caprice with two males pulled alongside and fired several rounds at the deceased victim with a shotgun and drove away toward Roosevelt."

"Looks like we have our first homicide of the night," James states to Cliff as they pull up on scene.

Cliff and James then proceed to process the scene as they have countless times before by relieving the rookie officers at the scene and taking control of the witnesses and crowds. As they are taking control, the officers begin to piece together information on the victim and a possible motive and then summon for the support units to begin processing the body and recovering the spent shells as evidence.

"Can anyone identify the deceased? His name? Address? Age? Relatives?"

"Does anyone have any descriptions of the shooter? His name, age or description? What about the car they were in?"

Back in the squad car, the two officers begin to combine their information and complete the necessary reports. Supporting units begin to arrive and do their respective duties.

"You know the one witness stated that the victim was a key witness in a trial set to begin next Monday…. My guess is he aint' gonna' testify" Cliff states.

"Yeah, that is the word on the street that I got. Remember that case we put together the year before last with the home invader that kept killing his victims? It's that guy's trial. I forget his name but I have the paperwork at the station" James continues.

Suddenly James and Cliff hear the sound of gunshots ringing out just a few blocks to the south of their location and look that way to notice a large cloud of smoke rising above the buildings. Within seconds, the radio begins to click again.

"Westside units, Westside units, several neighbors are calling in stating that there is a large fire at 20th and Trumbull. Neighbors are also reporting several shots being fired from the front and rear of that location and seeing a gray Chevy speeding away. No further information is available at this time," the dispatcher calls out for any available units to respond.

With the area being as busy as it is, no units are currently available as all are tied up handling various assignments.

"That sounds like the car described for our offender from this homicide," Cliff notes.

"Yeah, and that is also the same location where Xavier was shot last night. We should go check it out. We are done here anyway, the detectives can handle this." James tells Cliff as they leave their homicide to head toward the fire.

"What did we just get into?....."

"Westside 14." James calls over the radio to the dispatcher.

"Westside 14, go ahead with your transmission," Lynda responds hoping they will take the assignment of the fire.

"Westside 14, we'll go take a look at the fire since we are finishing up here and turn in all the paperwork in the station later," James responds as he accepts the assignment.

As the veteran officers pull up on the block of the fire, they observe a massive fire fully engulfing a two-story apartment building and what appear to be several motionless bodies sprawled across the front lawn. The neighborhood residents and passers-by have all stopped and have begun to form a moderate sized crowd.

"Westside14, this is a bon-a-fide fire and we need more units for crowd control. Send some ambulances as there are several people down at this location," Cliff orders over the radio as he and his partner are rushing toward the crime scene.

Once on-scene both officers once again begin to take control by ordering the crowd back and to make room for the Fire Department and their equipment when they arrive. Then Cliff hears his partner's voice over the radio.

"Westside 14, I need some Homicide Detectives over here and a supervisor. Do you copy?" James is requesting with a sense of urgency in his voice.

Hearing that transmission from his partner, Cliff understands that this is his partner's way of informing him that he has seen something out of the ordinary, and to gather as much information as possible. Officer Young then shifts modes from pushing the crowd away to make room, to an investigative mode by asking and gathering info from those willing to cooperate. Support units soon arrive and Cliff is able to again meet up with his partner to combine information.

"What did you see?" Cliff asks.

"The bodies, they have gunshot wounds. A concerned citizen motioned to me as we were running up by kicking at a shell casing on the sidewalk then looking at the victims. In the back is a gas can. That's why the house was fully ablaze when we got here. These victims didn't die in the fire. They were gunned down as they ran out." James explains.

"The homicide on Douglas, the arson and multiple homicides here, and a grey Chevy seen at both locations fleeing the scenes...Cliff, what did we just get into?" James asks his partner.

"I don't know...I don't know." Cliff responds shaking his head in disbelief.

"Let's finish getting the info on these victims and we'll do the report and figure it out at the station," Cliff answers.

Several hours have passed since the officers were assigned the fire and numerous support units have arrived and processed the scene accordingly. The remains of the four victims have been removed and taken to the coroner's office for processing and Officers Young and Robinson are now going to the station to finish up the paperwork.

At the station, the officers are looking over their paperwork from the drive-by shooting and the arson/ homicides checking for omissions and any errors when Cliff remembers to ask James for the old paperwork from the home invader. James then goes to his locker to get the file as Cliff continues to look for any other similarities other than the Chevy.

"DeRonn Johnson." James exclaims handing the file to Cliff as he returns from the locker.

"Now I remember the case!" Cliff exclaims as he looks the file over.

"Whoa, look. Look here." Cliff points in the file. They both then grab their current paperwork.

"Box 28, Witness Names. Andre Stack, Debra Stack, Marcus Stack, Darrell Stack, Deshawn Williams, and Priscilla Daniels" Cliff continues pointing out to his partner.

"Tonight's victims from the arson/ homicides.... the Stack Family," James states as he compares paperwork.

"And tonight's drive-by victim was Deshawn Williams. All are named witnesses in DeRonn Johnson's trial set for next Monday. The Stack family lived right where Officer Xavier first saw that guy in the alley last night. James, look in that file and tell me what's the physical description of DeRonn Johnson, the home invader." Cliff states as they begin to piece these cases together.

"Male, Black, 21 years old, 5 foot 11 inches, and 190 pounds," James states.

"It's a stretch, but, this very well could be the same guy that killed Officer Xavier last night, Deshawn Williams and the Stack family tonight. The one witness told us the trial starts next Monday and now the witnesses are all being killed. It might be a coincidence, but I don't think so. I think Xavier saw this guy in the alley last night behind the Stacks' apartment and interrupted him before he could kill them, that's when he got killed. So, now this guy has to finish the job before they testify against him," Officer Young explains.

"So, if that is the case, what about Priscilla Daniels? Could she be next? She has an address on the Boulevard. It's worth checking out" James explains as they both grab the file and open cases to make copies for themselves.

The two then look at one another sensing that they are onto something and state "What did we just get into?"

The Westside officers spend the rest of the tour pulling files and completing their preliminary investigations of the homicide and arson/homicides.

CHAPTER THREE: Sunday Night

"...I Aint' Going to Jail..."

The following day, Sunday night, both Officers Young and Robinson agree to meet at the station a few hours prior to the beginning of their tour to gather and assemble files.

"If we can piece all this together, we can let all the officers know what we are up against. James, I need to have copies of the old files for the home invasions and the arrest reports with pictures. I'll put the paperwork from Officer Xavier's homicide, the Williams boy's homicide, and Stack family homicides over here. We need to find out where DeRonn Johnson currently lives, and, who he hangs around," Officer Young continues to explain.

"As for Priscilla Daniels, we need to either get her under surveillance or into protective custody. If she is the missing piece, you can darn sure bet that he will be hunting for her."

Just as the veteran officers begin to piece the case together, their commanding officer walks in the room and notices the numerous files and pictures across the desk.

"You guys are here awfully early, do you need me to approve overtime? You're working a lead I take it?" the Lieutenant asks as he pulls up a chair.

"Forensic and ballistic results are in. The bullet that killed Officer Xavier was fired from the gun recovered on the side of that house. The prints recovered from the weapon turn out to belong to a Mr. DeRonn Johnson. The Detective Division forwarded me this info earlier today. I've made a copy of the file for you guys to look over and I'll keep the original in my office. Now what have you guys got?" asks the Lieutenant as he lays the copied results on the desk with the other files.

"That just proves our theory!" exclaims Cliff.

"James, try to pull this guy's criminal history while I explain this whole thing to the Lt.

The veteran officers then spend the remaining time prior to the start of their tour with the Lt. explaining the similarities and coincidences of these recent findings. Together, they have gathered enough information and evidence to seek a warrant for the immediate arrest of DeRonn Johnson.

"I want you two to explain your findings to the rest of the crew during roll call.   And hey, Good Job!" the Westside Command Lieutenant offers as he leaves the room to prepare for roll call.

In the Roll Call room, Officers Young and Robinson explain their findings and theories to their coworkers, passing out copies of the reports and files, as well as pictures of the wanted subject DeRonn Johnson. Officers Young and Robinson then turn the roll call back over to the Command Lieutenant.

The Command Lieutenant begins roll call by picking up where Officers Young and Robinson left off, explaining the findings of the ballistic and forensic tests, which were faxed to him earlier that day.

"Now back to business.   Officer Xavier's funeral arrangements will be posted on the board and all are expected to attend in formal uniforms. The wake will be held Tuesday from 0900 hours to 1900 hours....that is 9:00 A.M. to 7:00 P.M. for those who get confused with military time. We are asking for an Honor Guard to be present for the duration of the wake and funeral and need volunteers. Please see me after roll call to volunteer."

The Westside Command Lieutenant continues with roll call by calling out attendance and assignments, and dismissing the officers.

Not surprisingly taken, the Westside Command Lieutenant was overwhelmed with volunteers from his crew to serve as Honor Guard during the wake and funeral. The first of these officers to volunteer was the young officer from the locker room whom James confronted. Before long the whole block of times to serve was filled. Each officer's volunteering as way to show and pay their respect for their fallen coworker and friend.

As they leave the station and proceed to their squad car, Officers Young and Robinson begin to plan their agenda for locating DeRonn Johnson.

"Cliff, we have to hit DeRonn Johnson's last known hangouts. Grab and put pressure on his crew. Hopefully then, one of them will lead us to our man. According to his last arrests, he seems to keep being picked up in the vicinity of Roosevelt and Homan, with an address on Roosevelt."

"Yeah, true, but the address is bogus since that is now a parking lot. I am afraid that putting pressure on his crew might scare him off and into hiding. Plus the witness from the drive-by said that DeRonn had an accomplice who was driving the Chevy. There's no telling who that guy is, since no one got a good look at him." As the officers are discussing their plan, the dispatcher can be heard calling for them.

"Westside 14."

"Westside 14, Go ahead." Cliff responds.

"Westside 14, there is a suspicious person and auto at the corner of Douglas and Homan. The car is supposed to be playing a loud radio at that location. No further info is available at this time. Do you copy?"

"Westside 14, we copy." Cliff answers.

The two officers then proceed to the corner of Douglas and Homan just in time to see the taillights of a silver auto pulling away from the corner at a high rate of speed.

"Catch that car!"

"Westside 14," James calls out over the radio to dispatch.

"Westside 14, go ahead. You have the air."

"Westside 14, we are following a silver auto Westbound on Douglas from Homan. License plate of..6-3-9-F-R-S. Let the backup units know that the car is running all the lights, so be careful."

"Westside 14, the plate 6-3-9-F-R-S comes back as a stolen vehicle" the dispatcher responds.

"Westside 14, Emergency." James yells as his adrenaline begins to pump.

"We are now northbound on Independence... Eastbound on 13th Street...One male occupant.... approaching Central Park.... WE NEED BACKUP!!!!" James can be heard yelling as he continues updating the dispatcher of their location.

"Westside 14. He just turned into the dead-end alley. He's bailing out of the car from 13th and Homan, East alley."

Next, Cliff can be heard over the radio as they are now in a foot pursuit of the wanted offender. Running from yard to yard and vacant lot to lot they are slowly catching up to the offender.

"Westside 14, he's a male, black, late teens to early twenties, with a blue jersey and brown baggy jeans. We are eastbound through the gangway of approximately 1285 S. Christiana," Cliff radios.

"In the alley! In the alley!" James radios to let the responding units know where to go.

"Spaulding. 1283 S. Spaulding," Cliff yells as the offender continues to outrun the officers and turns the corner out of sight.

"James, do you see him?"

"No, he's taken up a hiding spot."

"Westside 12."

Officer Barnes' voice can be heard over the radio calling in an urgent tone.

"WESTSIDE 12" he emphatically calls out again.

"1283 S. Spaulding in the gangway. I have the offender!" Officer Barnes and his partner explain.

James and Cliff then run over to see Officers Barnes and Kelley in a life or death struggle with the offender who is refusing to give up. Meanwhile, the dispatcher can be heard over the radio sending units to their aid.

"I aint' going to jail," the auto thief explains as he continues to savagely punch and kick at the officers.

Together, Officers Barnes, Kelley, Young, and Robinson engage in a fierce battle with the muscular offender who is just as intent to not be apprehended, as the officers are to put him behind bars. As backup units begin to arrive on scene, the manpower overwhelms the offender and he is taken into custody.

Meanwhile, the dispatcher can be heard over the radio asking if everything was o.k.

"Westside 12? Westside 14? Any other units or officers who may have responded to 1283 S. Spaulding...Is the offender in custody? Are more units needed on scene?"

"Westside 12," Officer Barnes begins to answer back.

"Westside 12, go ahead."

"There are enough units on scene, and the offender is in custody. We will be going into the police station to process the arrest," Barnes continues to explain as he catches his breath and fixes his uniform and appearance.

"Westside 14."

"Westside 14," James answers still catching his breath.

"Westside 14, are you going to be held at the crime scene with the vehicle?"

"Westside 14, yes. We are inspecting the vehicle now. Can you confirm that the vehicle was stolen, and if so from who and where?"

Lynda responds "I'll put the information on your squad car's computer, do you copy?"

"Westside 14, we copy."

Cliff and James then begin to secure the crime scene for the support units and forensic investigators to process while they complete the required paperwork.

"James, you aren't going to believe this. The car's registered owner is Daniels. As in Priscilla Daniels," Cliff exclaims as he begins filling out the paperwork and retrieving the info from the computer.

"Does it give any contact info where she can be reached?" James asks.

"Don't see any as of yet. Check with dispatch for me."

"Westside 14, are there any contact numbers associated with this case?" James asks the dispatcher over the radio.

"Westside 14, that car was taken in during a home invasion and subsequent homicide. The owner of the car is also the victim. Do you copy?" Lynda responds.

"Westside 14, we copy."

"...Street Power..."

Officer's Young and Robinson are now trying to piece together whom this driver is and what role he has played in the events of the past several days. Their minds are racing a mile-a-minute. Have they caught Officer Xavier's killer?

Or could this be Priscilla Daniel's killer? Or is this just the driver of the getaway vehicle used in the Stack family and Williams' homicides.

While sitting in their squad car waiting for the detectives to arrive on scene, Officer Young notices a citizen motioning for his attention. Over the years, the officers have used the information given by this citizen to build many a case and in return they offer him a few dollars to eat.

"James, go check out what he wants for me while I complete this report."

"Yes sir. How may I help you?" James asks the man as he motions him to come closer.

"Act like you are arresting me, I have some info for you and your partner but I can't be seen talking with you freely," the older man states to the officer.

Officer Robinson then goes through the motions of an arrest and handcuffs the man.

"Cliff, open the door to the car. He's going in to the station for having a warrant."

James openly states as he places the man in the squad car in an attempt to mislead the watching citizens. As the detectives arrive, they then drive away from that area and talk to the citizen as he begins to relay the info he has overheard.

"You two are lucky to be alive right now. You do know that right?"

"What do you mean?" Cliff responds.

"Listen. Do you guys remember chasing a man a few nights back? Do you remember how he just disappeared and all you had was his sweatshirt? Well, it was a setup. A game of cat and mouse except you guys were about to become the mice. The guy you are looking for has been hiding out at that house on occasions. He is very arrogant and cocky. He is also a very high ranking gangster with street powers."

"Street power?" James asks.

"Street power. He rules like a king. What he says goes as law. Violate it, and the penalty is death, and death for your family. Other gang members are intimidated to the point that they have no choice but to obey him. I overheard him giving orders last Friday night that if anyone came to the house he was staying at, to shoot to kill. And that included the police. He then counted out five thousand dollars to each of about twelve of his enforcers and supplied them each with handguns."

"Why didn't you tell the police sooner?" Cliff inquires as he pulls the car over.

"Street power. Listen, I watched that man pass out orders, cash, and guns, like it was nothing to him. This man is known around the neighborhood for killing whole families when one member failed to obey. He does that just to prove a point. When you and your partner chased him back to that house, did you two notice how many people suddenly appeared as he disappeared?"

"Yeah, they did appear kinda' quickly," James notes.

"They all had guns and orders to kill. You and your partner were completely surrounded and didn't even know it. If either of you would have stepped further into that yard, neither of you would be here today. You both got lucky that all those other cops began showing up within seconds after that."

A brief pause is made in the man's speech as Officers Young and Robinson glance at each other realizing that they were almost ambushed.

"Like I said, cat and mouse. You thought you were the hunters, but you were almost hunted. Anyways, the man you are looking for uses the back entrance at that location. When he is there, he will have numerous fellow gang members acting as his security. They are ordered to protect the front and rear, and hang out on all of the surrounding porches and yards. And they have orders to "take out" anyone approaching that house. Anyone. You guys got lucky. Remember that. Let me out at the corner."

The officers then release the man and slip a twenty-dollar bill into his hand as they take the handcuffs off his wrists.

"You didn't hear any of this from me but DeRonn Johnson has the street power."

Officers Young and Robinson then head into the district station to finish the paperwork and to question the suspect arrested by Officers Barnes and Kelley.

"So that explains how the guy disappeared so quickly. All those other people acted as a diversion," Cliff states while thinking out loud.

"Yeah. Do you think we were really surrounded? We took up good positions as we approached and entered the yard. However, there were a lot of people out that night. Do you think we were walking into a trap?"

Both officers once again begin to replay the events that unfolded that fateful night. This time keeping in mind the new information they have been given and trying to see how it all fits in.

"You know, as we made the initial approach on the gangway, right after hearing the shot, I never saw anyone leaving the scene or hopping the rear fence. I only saw that guy in the yard after you said something," Cliff states.

"Yeah, that is when I first saw him. I noticed the movement in the yard. I never saw him leave from where Xavier was. Nor did I see how he got in that yard, I first saw him as I noticed him ducking down."

"That's just it! We must've seen him as he hopped the fence. If that fence is six feet tall, and DeRonn is five-foot-ten, we could not have seen him once he made it to the other side. But we both saw him in that yard, and we can't see through the wood panels. Therefore, the movement that we first noticed was him actually jumping down from atop the wooden fence," Cliff begins to explain.

"That is when we both ran over to notice him crouched by the side of the house. Exactly where the gun was later found. The same gun that was found to have DeRonn's prints on it. The same gun that was used to kill Officer Xavier," James continues.

"But, as we chased that guy, we saw him enter that yard. So my question is this, when did he have time to take off his sweater if we were right behind him, and all of us were running full speed? Furthermore, how could we let ourselves get surrounded without even noticing it?"

"It was as if we had tunnel vision. We were so focused on catching him; we excluded all other possible threats. I know for a fact that as I was scanning the crowd, anyone who did not resemble Deronn's height and weight was immediately dismissed as the killer. I was focused only on him, and didn't pay much attention to all those other people," Cliff notes.

"I was the same way. But he disappeared so fast; I just knew we had him. I just wanted him caught. I never even noticed all the people coming and standing around on the porches and in the gangways and alleyways until the dispatcher said to stop and let the dogs track the scent. It wasn't until then, while we were securing a perimeter and telling everyone to go back inside, that I noticed just how many people were actually out there," James adds.

"We were lucky. That will serve as a lesson learned. No matter what the situation, we should always pay attention to the actions of the crowd, and not be too focused on an individual," Cliff responds as they pull up into the station lot.

"Proof positive that tunnel vision kills."

In the station, Officers Barnes and Kelley are getting nowhere with their arrestee. The prisoner refuses to disclose any information at all and is not answering any questions.

"Look man, the sooner you give us your name and address, the sooner you can be booked, let's not make this an all night process. What is your name?" Officer Kelley asks.

"Your name?"

Still, not an utterance from his mouth. At this point both officers are ready to give up. Frustrated, Officer Barnes exits the interview room slamming the door.

"Wassup?" Cliff asks as he approaches Officer Barnes and hearing the door slam shut.

"Nothing, the guy will not speak a word. We can't get anything out of him. Not even a name."

"That is fine, just book him as a John Doe if he refuses, his fingerprints don't lie. You know that car belonged to Priscilla Daniels and was taken during a home invasion," James states.

"Yeah. We ran all the info on the computer once we got situated in the station. This guy has a lot of questions to answer, but he has not said a peep since we took him into custody. Nothing other than 'I aint' going to jail' and he said that on the street. The Detective division will be coming out to take over once we finish booking him so maybe they will have better luck," Barnes responds.

"Street power. He won't speak to them either" Cliff informs.

"Think about it. If someone was intent enough to fight the police to not go to jail and has been caught in a stolen car that was taken during a home invasion, don't you think they would want to make some kind of a deal? Not to mention that the car's owner is now dead! Come on. He should be grabbing at any break we threw his way. We just found out from a citizen that if he talks, not only will he be killed, but also his whole family is in danger of the same fate. He won't talk. So you might as well book him as John Doe. That is called street power."

The officers spend the rest of the tour completing their corresponding paperwork and being debriefed by the officers from the Detective Division. The offender refused to cooperate and was processed as John Doe.

CHAPTER FOUR: Monday Night

"...I Love You..."

It is now Monday night. Officer Young is standing in the bedroom mirror as he begins to get dressed for work. While he is checking his gear and preparing himself for work, his wife sits on their bed rocking their baby to sleep.

"The wake is in the morning for Officer Xavier. James and I will be doing the Honor Guard from three until four in the afternoon, so when I get home in the morning I will need to sleep for a few hours before I leave back out."

"That's no problem, I've got some running around to do anyway. I'll have the baby with me so you can get some rest. Honey, have you thought about leaving patrol?"

His wife asks as tears begin to well up in her eyes.

"It's just that I'm worried. I mean, I sit up night after night worried about you and James. All the while, I'm afraid. I sit here hoping, praying that you'll come home in the morning. Praying no one comes knocking at the door with bad news. Since this past Friday, I've been on edge every night. I, I, I sit here...."

His wife stops mid-sentence as she wipes away the tears that roll down her cheeks. With a wavering voice she looks at her husband and tries to continue.

"I sit here worrying, and afraid that one of these nights could be your last. I watch as you leave out the door, and I can't help but wonder how would I get along without you.

I try not to, but I do. I want our daughter to grow up and know her daddy, not stories about her daddy. Can you get off the streets and do something a little safer?"

Cliff turns from the mirror and looks over to his wife and sleeping daughter. He pauses, adoringly smiles and walks over to the bed. As he gently wraps his arm around his wife, he sits next to her on the bed in such a way that together they can both look at themselves reflected from the mirror.

"I love you."

Cliff reassures his wife as he reaches for some tissue and begins to wipe the tears from her eyes.

"Not only do I love you, but I am in love with you. Baby, you have made my life complete. You have given me all that I ever wanted or dreamed of. Every night when I walk out that door I pray. Do you know what I pray for?"

Cliff stops and wipes away more of her tears, then shifts from looking at the reflection and looks his wife in the eyes.

"I pray that I will not let down anyone that is counting on me. Especially my family, who is counting on me to be there for them. I know you worry about me, and I know how deeply you care. No matter what, I want you to know that I love you too, and I appreciate all that you do."

The two then embrace each other firmly and warmly. Cliff then wipes the tears from her eyes and kisses his wife and his daughter goodnight.

"Goodnight, I love you. I'll see ya' in the morning," Cliff again reassures his wife as he leaves for work.

"....Do It In Plain Clothes..."

At the station, Cliff sees James as he heads towards the Command Lieutenant's office. James motions for Cliff to follow him into the office.

"The Lieutenant wants to see us. He stopped me in the locker room while I was getting changed. 'Said to see him when you got here," James informs Cliff.

"Did he say what's up?"

"Nope. Just said to see him."

The two partners then proceed down the hall towards his office. Wondering what has transpired.

"Lieutenant, you wanted to see us?" Cliff asks.

"Yes. Come in and close the door. Take a seat."

"You guys talk to a citizen yesterday?" the Lieutenant asks.

"We always talk to people."

"You know who I am referring to. Anyways, he called the desk and wanted to talk to you two. 'Said he had some information about DeRonn Johnson, but would only talk to you. He said he wants to meet tonight, on the Boulevard at Homan Street."

"Lieutenant, this guy has been giving us good information for years. But, if anyone sees us talking to him they'll kill him. He's putting his life on the line to help us…"

"And you will meet him to find out all you can. You will do it in plain clothes and in an unmarked squad car," the Command Lieutenant demands as he interrupts James.

"Don't worry about being in roll-call, I know you are both here, so just go change into civilian clothing and get out there. Pick up your radios when you leave the office, and keep me informed as to what's going on."

"You got it, Lieutenant. Let's go James," Officer Young states as he taps his partner and pushes his chair back under the desk.

The two officers then leave the Command Lieutenant's office and sign out their police radios from the desk. As they head into the locker room to change from their uniforms back into civilian clothes the two wonder what information could be waiting for them. Anxious to find

43

out, the two hurry to change and do undercover work in the vicinity of Douglas Boulevard and Homan.

Over the next several hours the officers, posing as two drunks on the sidewalk, place themselves in a position where each can watch the alleged house of DeRonn Johnson. Each officer making mental notes as to where the gang members acting as his security are stationed. Before long the citizen from the previous night walks by. Both officers recognize him as he offers them some money.

"Here is a couple of bucks. Go and get a sandwich or something."

He hands the two officers several bills. One of which has writing on it. He then walks away, passing several of the gang members posing as security. Taking the money, the officers can see some writing on one of the bills. So as to not draw attention to the citizen informant from the security, the two officers then stagger away in the opposite direction.

Back in the unmarked vehicle, Officers Robinson and Young compare notes and read the message left on the money.

"It says here 'D.J. LEAVES TOWN AT 4 AM. USES FRIEND'S PICK-UP TRUCK HEADING TO GEORGIA'"

"We've gotta' act now! Call the Lieutenant and let him know we need more manpower to hit the house. Cliff, I counted two gang members on the porch of the house to the north, and two on the south. What about you?"

"There was also one across the street on the porch, and one at the corner we first passed, but I think he was just a lookout. It is now three o'clock that leaves us an hour to get this together. We will need some more officers to get to security and the lookouts before we can get close enough to the building."

Officer Young then pulls out his cell phone and begins to notify the Command Lieutenant.

"Lieutenant, this is Young. We met the citizen. He says that DeRonn Johnson is gonna' skip town in less than an hour. Gonna' use a friends pick-up truck to drive to Georgia. There are at least six gang members surrounding the house and unknown as to how many are in the house. It's Going Down Tonight! We need a team of at least ten uniformed officers to meet us around the corner to do this," Young states to the Command Lieutenant.

"Done. Meet in the parking lot of Roosevelt and Homan. Five minutes," the Lieutenant approves.

"Westside Command," the radio clicks as the Lieutenant calls for the dispatcher.

"Westside Command go ahead. You have the air," Lynda responds.

"Westside Command, have any available units in my command meet me at Roosevelt and Homan."

"Westside Command, we copy. Any available units are to respond to Roosevelt and Homan for a meeting."

"...BOOM, BOOM, BOOM..."

Within minutes, the parking lot has six units converged upon it. Each unit has two uniformed partners, with the exception of Officers Young and Robinson. Next the Lt. arrives, calling everyone to order and having Officers Young and Robinson detail out a plan of approach for the building and it's surrounding security.

At this point, each officer fully understands the seriousness to apprehend this man, and that they only have this one chance. Anticipation mounts, their hearts begin to beat fast, and the adrenaline pumps as the officers head back to their squads. They each pull out the parking lot and go to their respective corners and wait. Wait for Officers Young and Robinson to get into position and give the signal.

45

The two officers leave their unmarked squad car in the lot and begin to head back to where they were originally. As they get close, taking note of the positions of the gang members, they begin to swagger and stumble, as if both were actually drunk. Another agonizing ten minutes passes before both officers are in position. Meanwhile, the support units wait. The radios are silent. Volumes set to the minimum. The only sound heard in the squad cars is the slight hum of the engines. Then it happens.

A warning tone is repeatedly transmitted over the radio.

"That's it! GO, GO, GO!"

Officers converge from all directions. Completely taking the lookouts and security by surprise. Now it is Officer Robinson and Young's turn. The two jump up from their positions, and with Officers Barnes and Kelley, they rush the back door. Officer Young, the first to reach the rear door, runs full speed kicking the door open with his partner right behind him.

"POLICE. EVERYONE GET DOWN NOW!"

"GET DOWN, GET DOWN, GET DOWN."

Before the officers can all get into the house, numerous shots ring out. BOOM, BOOM, BOOM. A brief pause, then again, BOOM, BOOM, BOOM...BOOM, BOOM, BOOM, BOOM, BOOM, BOOM. Officer Young falls to the floor, then his partner.

"WESTSIDE 12, EMERGENCY. WESTSIDE 12, EMERGENCY!" Officer Barnes yells into the radio as he dives for cover.

"WESTSIDE 12, CODE 3. OFFICERS DOWN. 1737 W. HOMAN. WE NEED HELP NOW."

Looking over the banister and railing, Officer Barnes can see the two fallen officers as they are moving for cover. Struck in the chest three times and once in the arm, Officer

Young gasps for air as he calls out to his partner who was also struck by the gunfire.

"James."

"James, you o.k.?"

A moan, then a gasp for air. James looks over to his partner and confidently shakes his head.

"He's gonna' pay!" James responds to Cliff.

"Are you hit?" Cliff asks.

"Yeah, the vest stopped them. Hurts like hell..." James responds still gasping for air.

Suddenly they hear movement towards the front of the apartment. The two plain -clothes officers peek around the corner in just enough time to see the man they have been after for so long dash up the stairs. Officers from all around begin to converge on the house and set up a perimeter. Officers Barnes and Kelley finally make their way inside to provide backup for Cliff and James.

Slowly, Cliff and James make their way to the front staircase as Officers Barnes and Kelley make sure no one else is hiding on the main floor. The smell of gunpowder is strong and smoke and dust fills the air. All four officers make their way to the front slowly peeking up the staircase. Then a sound is heard. A sound that all easily recognize. The sound of an empty magazine clip dropping to the hardwood floors and the snap of a fresh magazine being loaded into the weapon.

At the top of the stairs he waits. Waiting for anyone to come around the banister at the bottom. Meanwhile, the dispatcher has been calling for anyone inside the building to answer his radio. Not getting any response, she continues to send more officers to the scene. At this point, the radio traffic is out of control with officers all trying to coordinate a rescue effort for the officers inside.

"Cliff, can you see anything from there?" James whispers.

BOOM, BOOM, BOOM, BOOM. Cliff jumps back as the gunman continues to fire rounds at the officers.

"Yeah, he is at the top of the staircase. Just as it turns at the top," Cliff answers.

"Officer Kelley, get on that radio and let the other officers know that they cannot get in here without becoming a target. DO IT!" Cliff orders.

Officer Kelley begins to man the radio and let the dispatcher and surrounding units know their situation. As he radios in the information numerous shots can be heard over the transmission. BOOM, BOOM, BOOM. More shots are fired trying to keep the officers at bay.

James screams as he jumps back.

"I'M HIT!!!"

He looks down at his shoulder as blood begins to trickle down his arm. Injured and enraged, Officer Robinson sends a barrage of bullets back up the staircase, with his partner providing cover. After about a minute of exchanging gunfire, the smell of gunpowder is extremely heavy and visibility is minimal from all the smoke and the darkness.

Still uninjured throughout the gunfight, DeRonn Johnson sits around the top of the staircase holding the injured officers at bay.

BOOM, BOOM, BOOM. He fires more rounds at the officers whenever he thinks they are coming. BOOM. The officers wait. Silence. For what seemed like an eternity, was only a minute. Then Deronn's voice is heard talking to the officers. A deep, rough, baritone voice calls out.

"I am coming down these steps and whoever is at the bottom will die!" DeRonn threatens.

The very sound of his voice makes the hairs on the back of the neck stand at attention. Their hearts, already beating a mile-a-minute skip a beat. Then the officers see a slight movement through the gun-smoke that has filled the hallway and staircase. Waiting, they see what first appears to be just a foot coming down the steps, but as they scan upwards, can see the profile of a person. Officers Young and Robinson each with a position on both sides of the staircase, injured, bleeding and still have not caught their breath, are soon to be face to face with Xavier's killer. As the killer makes his way to the turn at the top of the staircase he shoots. BOOM, CLICK, CLICK, CLICK. The weapon is now empty. Realizing this, the officers break from their covered positions and rush to the top of the stairs just as DeRonn dives back around the corner in an attempt to reload.

On the upstairs landing, DeRonn runs to the end of the hall with the empty weapon in hand. Now at the top of the stairs James and Cliff yell out orders.

"FREEZE."

"SHOW US YOUR HANDS... SLOWLY!" Cliff yells.

Slowly, the killer complies with the officer's commands by dropping the empty weapon to the ground. Cautiously, he raises his hands above his head. Just as he did in the back yard days earlier. Then DeRonn turns around and faces the officers, and with a smirk on his face, he laughs.

"GET ON YOUR KNEES. KEEP YOUR HANDS WHERE I CAN SEE THEM" James angrily orders.

"I give up. You got me. Good job," DeRonn mimics and laughs.

With his cocky and arrogant attitude he continues to taunt the officers.

"How long do you think it will take for me to get out this time? How long do you think it will take for me to find you? How long before I find your family. Or, maybe not me, maybe I'll order someone to do it for me. Good job. Now lock me up so I can call my lawyer."

There was a brief pause, then another cocky, arrogant, and taunting smirk.

BOOM.

CHAPTER FIVE: Tuesday

"...Daddy Has Wings Now...."

Clouds fill the sky and the rain gently falls to the ground as mourners continue to fill the already over-packed church. Outside, several hundred fellow officers are in rank and file formation standing at attention. All are adorned in formal uniforms with black mourning ribbons across their badges. They are lined up along both sides of the entrance, all the way to the street and to the corners of the church. As the rain drips from the brims of their caps and onto their faces, it seems to hide the tears that have welled up in their eyes. The melancholy mood becomes even more so as the black hearse makes its way slowly down the street, stopping in front of the packed church.

As the pallbearers remove the casket of the fallen officer from the hearse, all of the officers at attention salute in unison. The casket is slowly carried into the church to the pulpit area. As the casket is opened, and the flowers are being set in place, Amazing Grace can be heard being sung by the church choir. The officers are now in place for the Honor Guard. These officers stand at attention at both the head and foot of the body of their fallen comrade.

One by one, the members of Officer Xavier's family come up to the casket to pay their final respects and kneel to offer a prayer in his name.

"Xavier. Baby, I love you, and always have. Thank you for all you have done and given to our family. Your family. I will never forget you and I'll always love you."

His wife then leaves his side and returns to her seat in the front row, having now become overwhelmed with sorrow and grief.

"Mommy, is daddy an angel now?"

Xavier's four-year-old daughter asks.

"Yes. He's a guardian angel now. He protects us."

"Mommy, Daddy has wings now?"

"Yes. Daddy has his wings now."

As the last of the family members return to the front row, the multitude of friends that Officer Xavier has made over the span of his lifetime begin to make their way down the aisle. Each person taking a solemn moment to pay their respects and remember their friend in their own special way. Some left pictures, while others left cards. Some simply said their final goodbyes and held on to their own special memories. Each person mourned in their own way, showing their feelings in different ways.

The family and friends of Officer Xavier spent the majority of the day mourning the man they called Daddy, Husband, Son and friend. Many cried, some laughed recalling his happy spirit, and yet many more wanted answers. Why? Why Xavier, and not his partner? And at what cost? Soon those questions led to feelings of disbelief, and anger. Rage. Frustration.

Now, it is late in the afternoon and all available officers in the city's department have assembled outside the church. Many times more officers were present, than those who first assembled for the arrival of the hearse.

Slowly the processional of officers, now estimated at several thousand, take their turn paying their respects. State police, Sheriff's police, Suburban police, and some

Out-of-state officers all join the rank and file Chicago Officers in paying homage to a fallen brother.

After several hours of sitting before her husband's casket, the overwhelmed widow asks to be escorted outside for some fresh air. As the church doors opened and Mrs. Xavier exited the building, she was surprised to see literally thousands of officers from all kinds of departments standing at attention in their formal uniforms and lined up and down both sides of the street. The formations were at least fifteen rows deep. These officers were showing their dedication and respect for a fallen comrade in a steady downpour of rain.

Looking down the street at the outpouring of support, and visibly overwhelmed, Mrs. Xavier looks at the young officer as she releases his hand.

"Thank you."

"Thank you for your support. I appreciate you all." Mrs. Xavier states as the tears are now blending with the drops of rain on her face.

After a moment, Mrs. Xavier returns inside with a newfound sense of pride and gratitude for the family of men and women in blue, to which she belongs.

As the Reverend continues to officiate over the services, he takes a moment to recall a conversation he had with Officer Xavier.

"Officer Xavier came to me many years ago as a rookie seeking an answer to a question he had. He said 'Rev. I am wondering if this job is right for me. They give me this badge and this weapon and they train me for the worst-case scenario, but I question if I can ever use it to take another's life. Rev, I'm thinking about quitting." The Reverend states.

"I asked Officer Xavier a simple question. I asked him if he knows of a righteous man who stands for a righteous cause, and has he ever seen the righteous forsaken?"

"From that day I knew he was going to be a good cop. A cop with morals and respect, coupled with integrity and a righteous heart. Officer Xavier chose to defend the defenseless, be a role model and ultimately died for a cause he believed in. But, now I ask you, have you ever seen the righteous forsaken?"

The Reverend continues with the eulogy and finishes the services just as the rain ceases, almost to symbolize a passing of troubled times. The Reverend closes by taking note of the afternoon sun as it begins to peek through the storm clouds. The rays of sunshine light up the inside of the church as they pass through the stained glass.

"The heavens shall cry no more, for the light has come."

At that moment, the choir begins to uplift the congregation by singing and swaying and clapping. Before long, numerous persons amongst the congregation have joined in. Outside, a final tribute is done in the form of a twenty-one-gun salute as Taps is played.

Later that day, Mrs. Xavier arrives at the hospital to visit Cliff and James. Recovering in their hospital room, they were unable to attend the services for their fallen coworker and friend.

"Hello?" She whispers as she knocks at the door.

"Come in." James replies as he sits up in the bed and moans.

"How do you guys feel?"

"We'll be fine. The doctors did a good job during the surgeries I hear. Cliff's still groggy from the anesthesia, coming in and out. I came out of surgery around noon. Had all day to myself. Sorry we missed the services. It was all over the news. Impressive." James adds.

"Yes. I will never forget what you have done for my husband and family. I just wanted to say thank you in person. It really means a lot to me."

"We got him." Cliff reassures Mrs. Xavier as he awakens.

"I heard."

Mrs. Xavier then leans over and kisses Cliff's forehead as she adjusts his sheets.

"I can't thank you and James enough. You two are my heroes. My husband and I are forever thankful."

"You know, today I saw a miracle. Today as I stood on the church steps during the services, I saw men and women from all over the state and from different parts of the country stand and salute to a fallen comrade. I saw men and women of all different races and nationalities paying their respects to a man whom many had never before seen or known. Through the rain, I saw the tears in their eyes as they stood in formation. But besides all that, do you know what I saw? I saw that I have the greatest family standing besides me and shoulder-to-shoulder with me. And for those men and women, I say THANK YOU."

As Mrs. Xavier wipes the tears from her face with a tissue, she leans over to adjust the bed sheets for James and kisses his forehead. She replaces the tissue in her purse as she leaves the room.

CHAPTER SIX: Fourteen Months Later

"...I Saw An Officer Die..."

As day four of the criminal trial begins, numerous officers assigned to the Westside district sit, waiting to be called to testify. The mood is tense. Each officer understands their testimony will be needed to convict the accused murderer of their friend and coworker Officer Xavier. The tension magnifies as yet another officer is called to enter the courtroom. Packed to capacity, the courtroom is dead silent with everyone in attendance waiting and intently listening to the District Attorney. Confident and well versed, the prosecuting attorney for the State against DeRonn Johnson leads the case and controls the tempo of the courtroom.

"Prosecution now calls Officer Cliff Young to the stand."

The sheriff leads Officer Young from the witness room to the main entrance of the courtroom. Officer Young opens the door to see all heads turned his way, as he is now the center of attention. As he makes his way down the center aisle he notices the majority of those in attendance are fellow officers in full uniform and Xavier's surviving family. Just across the aisle are the greatly outnumbered family and friends of DeRonn Johnson. As Officer Young takes the stand, a deafening silence takes over the courtroom.

"Please stand and raise your right hand," the stern faced judge states.

"Do you solemnly swear that the testimony that you are about to give, will be truthful, so help you God?"

"I do." Officer Young confidently states, and turns to take his seat.

The prosecuting attorney then continues his masterful presentation and questioning which he and his team of fellow attorneys have planned for over a year.

"Officer, Please give your name and district of assignment for the record."

Officer Young turns to the jury box, making direct eye contact with the jurors and the attorney and answers "Officer Cliff Young, assigned to the Westside district."

"I want to introduce a tape recording of radio transmissions from that eventful night as Exhibit A."

The District Attorney then picks up the tape recorder and purposefully places it on the ledge of the jury box, right in front of the jurors. He slowly adjusts the volume to the maximum and then presses the play button. There was a slight pause, then, voices resonate throughout he courtroom.

"......EMERGENCY.... Westside 13, Westside 13, EMERGENCY....." The courtroom is silent as the tape continues to play the voice of the fallen officer in his last moments of life.

"... Westside 13, EMERGENCY!!.... Man with a gun.... Westside 13, we are being shot at. My partner is in foot pursuit..." as the prosecutor identifies the voices within the transmissions for the jurors, the tape continues to play.

"CODE 3, CODE 3, there is a CODE 3 at 20th and Trumbull.... Westside 13?...Westside 13, He's a male, black, about 23 years old, black hooded sweatshirt, blue jeans, just ducked between the houses in the gangway..."

Click.   The prosecutor stops the tape then repeats the description as he addresses the jury.

"Ladies and gentlemen of the jury Officer Xavier has just stated over their police radios that the person who just shot at he and his partner is a male.... black...about 23 years old.... with a black hooded sweatshirt and blue jeans. Officer Young, when you responded to assist Officer Xavier on that eventful evening, did you by chance observe anyone fitting that description?"

"Objection!" The defense attorney blurts out. "Many people can fit that description."

"Sustained" The judge interrupts "Rephrase the question."

"Officer Young, did you in fact respond to assist Officer Xavier and his partner Officer Baker that evening?"

"Yes."

"And will you describe who or what you were looking for when you arrived on scene?"

"I was looking for Officer Xavier and his partner, Officer Baker. I was also looking for anyone who may have matched the description given by Officer Xavier over the police radio, with that description being a male, black, about 23 years old, who may have been wearing a black hooded sweatshirt and blue jeans."

"And, Officer Young, upon your arrival what did you find?"

"Upon initial arrival, I found the squad car assigned to Officer Xavier and his partner, unsecured, with several windows shot out, and numerous bullet holes in the side. But I had to ask over the radio for further assistance in locating either officer."

The prosecuting attorney continues to maintain and control the tempo as he walks back over to the tape recorder sitting on the ledge of the jury box.

"I warn you all that this next section of audio is very graphic," he states as he pushes the play button.

".... Westside 14, we are on scene at 20th and Trumbull, where are the officers?.... Westside 13, you have Westside 14 on scene where are you?...We are in the gangway at approximately BOOM!!!...CODE 3, EMERGENCY CODE 3!!! OFFICER DOWN, GET ME SOME HELP OVER HERE!!! ROLL ME AN AMBULANCE, CODE 3!!!!" the prosecuting attorney stops the tape as numerous people throughout the courtroom react to hearing the gunshot that ended Officer Xavier's life.

"Now, Officer Young, could you take a moment to describe the next couple of minutes in your own words."

"I remember hearing the gunshot both over the radio and a few doors away. My partner and I ran toward the sound of the gunshot and found Officer Baker holding Xavier in the gangway. Officer Baker was pointing, motioning for us to pursue the offender who was running from the rear across the alley."

"Officer Young, did you see the offender at that time?"

"Yes. Just as he was hopping the fence."

"Who did you see hopping the fence and fleeing the scene of the crime?"

"I saw a male, black, about 23 years old, with a hooded sweatshirt and jeans."

"Did you see anything else, Officer Young?"

"I saw an Officer die!"

Realizing the emotional impact that Officer Young's last statement would have on the jury, the attorney pauses questioning for a brief moment.

"Officer, did you pursue that person?"

"Yes, my partner and I immediately began pursuit by approaching the fenced-in yard that the suspect had just entered."

"And what happened next?"

"We managed to gain a position in which we could see the offender crouched down by the side of a house."

"Objection! Judge, this officer is testifying for both he and his partner" the defiant defense attorney exclaims.

"Sustained. Please refer only to your testimony. Your partner will be called to testify for himself," the judge corrects.

"I gained a position in which I could see the offender crouched down by the side of a house," Officer Young restates.

"At this time, Officer, were you able to see the face of the person crouched?"

"Yes, when my partner ordered him to 'Freeze and show his hands' the offender looked back in my direction." Officer Young confidently asserts.

"Is that person in the courtroom today?"

"Yes." Officer Young then looks over to the Defense and glares at DeRonn Johnson.

Pointing, Officer Young states "DeRonn Johnson was the man I saw that night."

Continuing with the tactful mastery of bring forth the facts, the Prosecuting attorney continues the questioning.

"Officer Young, were you able to apprehend Mr. Johnson that night?"

"No."

"What prevented you from apprehending Mr. Johnson?"

"After refusing to comply to the verbal instructions he was given, DeRonn Johnson then ran from my partner and I as we were attempting arrest. After chasing DeRonn Johnson through numerous yards and for several blocks he managed to remove the black hooded sweatshirt that he was wearing and hide."

"Officer Young, to the best of your knowledge, would you please tell the court what if anything was recovered from the spot you first saw DeRonn Johnson." The prosecuting attorney asks.

"To the best of my knowledge, a support unit with a canine team searched that yard and recovered a loaded revolver with one spent shell casing" Officer Young states.

"And, Officer Young, to the best of your knowledge, would you please tell the court whether or not the weapon was tested for DNA and fingerprint evidence."

"Yes it was. To the best of my knowledge the forensic evidence lifted from the weapon and the shell casings matched exactly with those on file belonging to DeRonn Johnson."

"Officer Young, you testified that the offender you were chasing that night 'removed a black hooded sweatshirt that he was wearing' and hid from you and your partner. Whatever happened with that sweatshirt?"

"To the best of my knowledge it was recovered by the evidence technicians on scene processed as evidence. I was later notified by the detectives that hair samples in the hood of the sweatshirt was tested for DNA and compared to those in the database."

"Officer, were you given the results of those tests?" the prosecutor asks having already obtained the answer.

Officer Young confidently assures the jury by stating "The DNA obtained from the sweatshirt of the man I was chasing that night matched that of DeRonn Johnson."

"At this time, I have no more questions for this officer, and would like to recall this witness at a later time."

DeRonn Johnson sits across the courtroom and offers a cocky and confident smirk as his attorney rises and approaches the jury box for cross-examination.

"Officer, you testified that you saw a male, black, about 23 years old, wearing a hooded sweatshirt and jeans. Is that correct?"

"Yes."

"You also testified that you first saw that person as he hopped a fence. Is this also correct?"

"Yes."

"Officer Young, on the night in question, about how far were you from that fence?" The defense attorney asks trying to nip away at the Officer's testimony.

"I was about forty-five feet away from the fence."

"And the very next time you saw my client was when you approached the fence that my client supposedly hopped?" asks the defense attorney.

"Yes."

"Officer Young, you testified that you saw my client's face when he looked back at you and your partner. Where was he when that happened, and where were you?"

"He was in the yard directly across the alley from the homicide scene, crouched down by the side of the house, where the weapon was recovered. I was in the alley at the fence."

The defense attorney smirks and asks "Oh, so you were on one side of the fence and my client was on the other side. Is that correct?"

"Yes!" Officer Young defiantly asserts trying to understand the point of his questioning.

"Officer Young, would you be so kind as to describe the fence that my client allegedly hopped that night."

"It is a six foot high wooden plank fence," Officer Young states.

" Officer, how tall are you?"

"I am 5 feet 11 inches tall."

"Hmmm, that's weird. I mean, how is it possible for you, at only 5' 11 inches manage to see over a fence that is 6 feet tall and still see a man 'crouching down' in the yard...Or maybe you were able to see through a fence made of wood planks. And do it in the darkness of night!!! I bet that's something they teach in the academy, huh? No more questions at this time."

After Officer Young steps down from the witness stand the judge adjourns court until the following morning.

Day 5 of DeRonn Johnson's murder trial is spent hearing testimony from the officers assigned to the Canine Unit, the Evidence Technicians, and the Forensic Lab Specialists. DNA, and fingerprint evidence is introduced and surprisingly goes unchallenged by the defense.

"...You Only Know HALF The Story..."

Day 6, sensing the team of defense lawyers have a trick up their sleeve, the prosecuting attorney calls Officer Robinson to the witness stand. Wearing the formal uniform with awards and medals adorning his chest, Officer Robinson enters the courtroom with a commanding presence.

"Officer, please raise your right hand to be sworn in."

"Do you solemnly swear that the testimony that you are about to give, will be truthful, so help you GOD?"

"I do."

"Officer, please state your name and district of assignment for the record."

"I am Officer Robinson, currently assigned to the Westside district."

The prosecuting attorney takes a moment as he walks the courtroom floor with the commanding stage presence like that of a veteran actor. As he approaches an oversized picture of the gangway with a view towards the rear alley and wooden fence he picks up a pointer and directs the officer and jury's attention toward it.

"Officer Robinson, do you recognize this photograph?" the prosecuting attorney begins.

"Yes. That photo looks like a depiction of the homicide scene," Officer Robinson states.

"Objection! Your Honor, that photo could have been taken from anywhere in the city, county, or even the state!" the defense attorney defiantly asserts.

"Sustained."

Almost as if he had expected an objection to the picture, the States Attorney in one smooth motion simply slides the picture to the right, revealing a second oversized picture. This second picture shows the exact same depiction as the first with one exception. Taken with a wider angled camera, the address is clearly visible.

"Officer Robinson, does this picture look familiar to you?" the states attorney confidently continues.

"Yes. That picture also depicts the homicide scene."

"And Officer, would you please note the numbers attached to the wall. Do they represent the same address as the homicide scene?"

"Yes."

"So it is safe to say that these two pictures are, in fact, taken from the same scene?" the prosecution continues.

"Yes, it is."

"Officer, would you please come over here and point out where you first noticed Officer Xavier, and where you first saw anyone fleeing the scene."

Officer Robinson calmly, and professionally begins to answer the prosecuting attorney's questions by taking the pointer and intentionally directing the answers to the members of the jury.

"Officer Xavier was lying motionless in his partners arms right here. And, from this angle I could see the offender as he was climbing this gate."

"And, Officer Robinson, did you give chase to that offender?"

"Yes. My partner and I both pursued the offender. As we approached the fence that the offender had just climbed, we were able to see him crouching by the side of a house," Officer Robinson continues.

"Objection! Your Honor, this officer is also trying to give testimony for both he and his partner" the defense claims.

"Sustained. Please refer only to your own experiences and testimony," the judge warns.

"OK, I was able to see the person who had just hopped the fence crouched down by the side of the house!!!" Officer Robinson corrects.

"Could you describe for the court the physical description of that offender?"

"He was a male, with a black hooded sweatshirt and jeans."

"A male, with a black hooded sweatshirt and jeans. This Officer has just described for the court who he personally saw flee the scene of a homicide. This officer is testifying to the exact same description, and the exact same location, as the man Officer Xavier described in the radio transcripts just seconds before his own murder."

Turning his attention directly to the jury, the States Attorney directs Officer Robinson back to the witness stand and continues to address the jury.

"Ladies and gentlemen of the jury, you have heard testimony from several officers over the past several days. You have heard individual accounts repeatedly placing that man, DeRonn Johnson, at the scene of the crime, committing the crime, and fleeing the scene of the crime. You have seen the black hooded sweatshirt, and the gun. Both were left behind as the offender fled from pursuing officers. Yesterday, ladies and gentlemen, officers specifically trained in evidence detection and recovery testified. You heard their testimony. You know now that DNA from the sweatshirt matches DeRonn Johnson. You now know that the fingerprints from the gun match DeRonn Johnson. But you only know HALF the story!!!"

Having gotten the full attention of the jury members and leaving them with a thirst for more, the prosecuting attorney turns back to the officer.

"Officer, we know that the person who was in that yard escaped being captured that night. Were you able to establish his identity."

"Yes. Within days, we the members of the Chicago Police Department, were all directed to be on the lookout for DeRonn Johnson, 'wanted for the murder of a Chicago Police Officer. Officer Xavier."

"Officer Robinson, I want you to recall the events leading to the capture of DeRonn Johnson. Please, take a moment. 'Ladies and gentlemen of the jury, the second half of the story starts with a manhunt, and ends with a shootout.' Officer Robinson, knowing the identity of whom you were looking for, what did you do?" the prosecutor cunningly asks setting up his next phase of questioning.

"Well, through the use of neighborhood informants, I was able to ascertain the current whereabouts of DeRonn Johnson."

"My partner and I met the informant in civilian clothes at an undisclosed location and he gave us an address to watch, and information that DeRonn was going to skip town within hours using a friend's truck."

"Did you act on this information, and if so what did you do?"

"I, along with my partner, called for backup, and organized a plan to place the offender into custody" Officer Robinson states.

On the prosecution's table is the tape recorder. The States Attorney, purposely motions toward the recorder. Picking it up and adjusting the volume, he walks toward the jury box. Again, situating it on the ledge for maximum effect.

"I would like to introduce the police radio tapes from that night. Now, Officer, when backup arrived, did you return to the address you were given?"

"Yes. I, along with my partner, were posing as two drunken bums on the street. We returned to the address and set up a position where we could see the house and its surroundings."

"And how long would you say it took for you and your partner to do that?"

"About ten to twenty minutes passed before we gave the signal."

The prosecuting attorney then presses the play button. A slight pause, then the warning tone is heard. Another slight pause then voices fill the courtroom. Voices of fellow officers yelling with a sense of urgency for more help, grip their attention like a dog to a bone.

"WESTSIDE 12, EMERGENCY. WESTSIDE 12, EMERGENCY. WESTSIDE 12, CODE 3. OFFICERS DOWN. 1737 W. HOMAN. WE NEED HELP NOW."

"Do you recognize that voice?" the attorney asks as he pauses the tape for a moment.

"Yes. That was Officer Barnes."

"Officer, on the tape, we all just heard that officer screaming for help and that there were officers down. Who were the officers down he was referring to?"

"Those officers were myself and Officer Young, my partner."

"Will you please describe for the jury the circumstances?" the prosecutor leads in questioning.

"Officer Young and I were situated close to the door at the address, waiting for DeRonn Johnson to come out. When the door opened and I had visual confirmation of the offender I gave the signal. That was the signal you heard on the tape, and, that was when we attempted to apprehend Mr. Johnson. Officer Young was the first to the door. I was second. Officer Young kicked the door in as Mr. Johnson fled into the house. Mr. Johnson then fired several shots at us as he fled to the top of the stairs. Officer Barnes was behind me and saw us as we were struck by the gunfire."

"Did you return fire?"

"Not at that time. I was shot in the chest, and needed to find cover. I took a moment to focus and catch my breath, then to see if my partner was o.k. He was struck three times in the chest and once in the arm, and also knocked out of breath, clambering to get out of the line of fire. Once DeRonn Johnson made it to the top of the stairs, he reloaded and began to fire at will at us. That is when I returned fire."

"It says in the report, that you were struck a second time, this time in the shoulder. Is that also correct?" the States Attorney leads.

"Yes. As we approached the bottom of the stairs."

"And did you see who shot you?"

"Yes. DeRonn Johnson. He then stated that he was 'coming down these steps and whoever was at the bottom will die" Officer Robinson states.

"Officer, did Mr. Johnson know who was at the bottom of his steps?"

"Yes!!! My partner and I both repeatedly ordered him to give up saying that we were the police. He was able to hear our commands, the radios, and see the uniforms of all the assisting officers."

"Please inform the court as to what let to his arrest."

Officer Robinson then turns to the jurors and continues. "As Mr. Johnson made his way down from the top of the stairs, he pointed his weapon at Officer Young and pulled the trigger several times. The first time fired a shot, then we heard 'CLICK, CLICK, CLICK. All of us realized that his gun was empty at the same time. DeRonn Johnson turned and ran back up the stairs, and, Cliff and I chased after him. He was placed into custody on the second floor hallway."

"Your Honor, I have no more questions."

The States Attorney then returns to his seat and gathers his notes as the Defense Attorney for DeRonn Johnson approaches the stand.

"Officer, you testimony seems to stop a little short of the truth. I mean, after you allege that my client shot you and your partner numerous times, how did you feel. Revenge, would never have crossed your mind would it? When you ran to the top of the stairs and found my client on his knees with his hands in the air, you shot him in his chest anyway. How did it feel?"

"OBJECTION!!!" The whole team of Prosecuting attorneys state.

"Sustained. Defense do you have specific questions for this witness?" the judge asks banging the gavel.

"We have nothing further Your Honor."

"Fine then, Officer Robinson, you may step down. Prosecution you may call your next witness."

"...Do You Know Who Shot Mr. Johnson?..."

"Prosecution would like to recall Officer Young to the stand" the States Attorney states as he approaches the center of the courtroom floor. After a few brief moments the doors open as Officer Young returns to the witness stand.

"Officer, please remember that you are still under oath," the judge reminds.

"Officer Young, I need you to recall the events leading to the arrest of Mr. DeRonn Johnson. Do you recall entering the house?"

"Very clearly." Officer Young states glaring at Mr. Johnson as he still sits confidently in his chair.

"In your own words will you describe what led you to enter the house?"

"We, meaning my partner and I, had obtained information that Mr. Johnson was at that house. We set up surveillance and positioned ourselves to be able to make an arrest."

"And Officer, what made you enter the house?" the Prosecuting Attorney leads in questioning.

"I saw Mr. Johnson when he opened the door, and attempted to make the arrest with my assisting officers. DeRonn Johnson fled back into the house shutting the door behind him."

"And how did you manage to get inside the residence?"

"I kicked in the door while in direct pursuit of Mr. Johnson."

"Then what happened, in your own words?" leads the prosecution.

"As the door opened I was shot three times in the chest and once in the arm as I fell to the ground. My partner, Officer Robinson who was right behind me, was struck in the chest when I fell."

"Did you see the man trying to kill you and your partner?"

"DeRonn Johnson, the man sitting at the table right there" Officer Young angrily points out to the jury.

"Now Officer, did you ever identify yourself to Mr. Johnson?"

"Absolutely. When we broke cover and approached the residence I was yelling 'POLICE. POLICE EVERYONE GET DOWN.'"

"And Officer, to your knowledge, is there anyway that Mr. Johnson could not have known that you were the police?"

"NO! He knew. He heard me, saw me, and ran. He saw my partner, he heard the commands, and he heard our radios. DeRonn Johnson knew the police were looking for him. He knew we were at his door and he fired at us." Officer Young assures the jury.

"Did you return fire at Mr. Johnson?"

"I first sought shielding from the barrage of bullets he was firing at us. As we approached the stairway, I was able to return fire."

The attorney pauses. Flipping through his notes he recalls a statement from the earlier testimony of his partner.

"Says here, 'I am coming down these steps and whoever is at the bottom will die.' Do you remember anyone saying that? And, who were they referring to?"

"I do remember Mr. Johnson saying that from the top of the stairs, just after he shot my partner in the shoulder."

"Officer, was DeRonn Johnson injured at any point of prior to his arrest that night?"

"Yes. At some point during the exchange of gunfire he was shot in the chest."

"Do you know who shot Mr. Johnson?"

"NO. There were so many shots being fired and so much gun-smoke, that I cannot say."

"And lastly, Officer, was there a gun recovered at the scene the night of Mr. Johnson's arrest."

"Yes. Mr. Johnson dropped the weapon to the ground when I ordered him to 'show his hands.'"

"I have no more questions."

"Defense, your witness," the judge directs.

"We have no questions at this time Your Honor," the defense relates.

"If the State has no more witness to call at this time, then we will adjourn for the evening."

The judge then dismisses Officer Young from the witness stand and adjourns court until the next morning. As Day seven begins, jurors hear testimony from more Forensic Experts, Evidence Technicians, and DNA Experts. The whole first half of the day is spent presenting evidence from the recovered bullets from the officer's vests, and the recovered weapon at the time of arrest. Again, the Defense makes no attempt to refute this evidence. Shockingly, the Defense Attorney for DeRonn Johnson stands ready to call him to the stand after the State rests their case.

CHAPTER SEVEN: Has The Jury Reached A Verdict

"...Did Anyone Ask?....."

The second half of day seven has now begun as the judge, jury, team of prosecutors, and team of defense attorneys have all returned to the courtroom sensing the end of the trial is fast approaching. The mood is light, as both sides seem to be more relaxed.

"Does the State wish to call anymore witnesses?" the judge asks the team of prosecutors.

"No. The State rests its' case."

"Then does the Defense wish to call any witnesses?"

"Yes, Your Honor the Defense would like to call DeRonn Johnson to the stand at this time."

Suddenly, the mood becomes a bit more serious as the jurors, and prosecutors anxiously await the coming testimony. DeRonn smiles at his lawyer as he rises out of his chair and adjusts his suit jacket. Confidently, he walks towards the witness stand and gives an arrogant smirk at the team of prosecuting attorneys as he passes.

"Mr. Johnson, please raise your right hand."

"Do you solemnly swear that the testimony that you are about to give will be truthful, so help you God?"

"Yes."

DeRonn then takes a seat in the witness stand again showing the arrogant smile and not appearing to be worried about the outcome. The Defense now takes its turn in proving their client's innocence.

"Sir, please state your name for the record" the Defense starts.

"I am Mr. DeRonn Johnson."

"Now Mr. Johnson, you have been charged with murdering a police officer, several counts of attempted murder of police officers, obstruction, and unlawfully possessing a weapon. For the record, at the time of your arrest, did you give any statement to the investigating officers?" the Defense begins.

"No, when the police arrested me, they shot me first and the next thing I knew I was being taken to the hospital for surgery. When I woke back up, they told me that I was under arrest and charged with murder."

"Did anyone ask you to explain your side of the story before they charged you?"

"No."

The defense attorney turns toward the jurors and begins.

"The Prosecution stated earlier in the trial that only half of the story was being heard. They were right! They never asked for your version. They just went on what they assumed to be the truth, and charged accordingly. Well, it is my job to expose the other side of the story. The other half that the State somehow left out."

"Mr. Johnson, let's turn your attention to the night that Officer Xavier was shot to death. Do you remember where you were that evening?"

"Yes. I was visiting a friend and his family directly behind the gangway from where the officer was shot." DeRonn explains.

"Mr. Johnson, in your own words would you please explain what you heard or saw that evening?"

"Sure. While I was visiting with Mr. Michael Catchings and his family, I heard a gunshot. I looked in the direction from where the shot was heard and I saw a hand reach over the fence and throw a black object into the yard," Mr. Johnson explains.

"Did your friend also see that happen?"

"I don't know. I remember that he was rushing his family inside the house."

"Mr. Johnson, what happened next?"

"I went over to see what was thrown into the yard. I saw that it was a gun and as I picked it up, two officers began to yell at me."

"Would you please explain to the jurors the reason you picked up that weapon."

"Because, like I said, I was visiting the family, and they have two young children. I did not want them to get hurt," DeRonn begins to explain.

"Now, Mr. Johnson, just to clarify for the rest of us, is it your testimony that you picked up the gun because there was a reasonable possibility that a young child would find it laying in the yard that they play in?"

"Yes."

"Mr. Johnson, please explain what happened when the police arrived at the rear fence."

"They were pointing their guns at me and yelling all sort of orders. As I stood up I dropped the gun back to the grass and raised my hands high. But, when I looked back, I saw those guns and got scared, so I ran."

"You ran because you were scared. Ladies and gentlemen of the jury, I need you to place yourselves in my client's position. You are visiting a family with young children, you hear a gunshot, and see a weapon being tossed into the yard where the kids are playing. As you attempt to move the weapon out of the reach of children, the police approach you with guns pointed at you and yelling orders.

You would be scared too! My client was scared so he ran. Ladies and gentlemen we do not refute the fact that the prints lifted off the gun belonged to my client. My client was only trying to do the right thing by moving it to a safer place until the police could arrive."

Turning his attention back to Mr. Johnson, the Defense attorney continues his questioning.

"Turning your attention to the night you were arrested, do you recall those circumstances?"

"Yes."

"Please explain to the jury what you remember about that night."

"I remember opening my door to go outside. Suddenly, these two men jumped up and yelled 'GET HIM.' I remember seeing guns in their hands as they were running towards me. I only had enough time to run back into the house and slam the door shut before it was being kicked in by those guys. I thought they were going to kill me, so I grabbed my gun and shot them as they entered my house. I did not know they were police."

"But they had on easily recognizable uniforms right?" the Defense attorney inquires.

"No. I thought they were two bums from the neighborhood. They were wearing dirty jeans, and ripped shirts."

"Ladies and gentlemen, did you hear what my client has just told you? He said that he thought two people were after him. These two people ran at him with guns, and kicked in the door to his house while yelling 'GET HIM.' These two people were not in the uniforms recognized as police, but rather, dirty jeans and ripped shirts. So he defended himself like anyone would."

"Now Mr. Johnson, did you realize that those two people were in fact actual officers before or after you attempted to defend yourself?" the Defense inquires.

"After. It was after several minutes of exchanging shots at one another. When I realized that they were police, I gave up. And that's when they came up the stairs and shot me."

"Mr. Johnson, did you shoot Officer Xavier?"

"No!" DeRonn Johnson states.

"Were you present when Officer Xavier was shot?"

"No! I was visiting Mr. Catchings across the alley."

"Mr. Johnson, did you knowingly shoot, or attempt to kill any officer of the Chicago Police Department?"

"No!"

"I have no more questions for this witness at this time," the Defense attorney states.

"Prosecution, your witness" the judge directs.

"No questions at this time Your Honor" the Prosecution asserts relying on their solid case.

"You may step down Mr. Johnson. Call your next witness" the judge directs the Defense team.

"Your Honor we would like to call Mr. Michael Catchings to the stand."

After a short pause in the courtroom, a court deputy escorts a young man in from the hallway. The jurors notice his demeanor as he enters. Appearing to be either shy or frightened he approaches the witness stand. Mr. Catchings never looks toward his friend, or toward the jurors.

"Please raise your right hand. Do you solemnly swear that the testimony that you are about to give will be truthful so help you God?"

"Yes."

As Mr. Catchings goes to his seat on the witness stand the jurors notice his shaking hands as he sits.

"Sir, would you please state your name for the record?" the Defense begins.

"Michael Catchings."

"And, Mr. Catchings, how do you know my client Mr. DeRonn Johnson?"

"We are neighborhood friends," Mr. Catchings nervously answers.

"I would like for you to recall your attention to the night of the shooting of Officer Xavier. Do you recall that night?"

"Yes."

"Do you remember having any company over?" the Defense inquires.

"Yes. DeRonn was visiting me and my two children."

"Do you remember hearing any gunshots that night?"

"Yes. The four of us were in the back yard when we heard one shot from the building behind us across the alley."

"In your own words Mr. Catchings, would you please describe what happened next?"

"Like I said, we were in the back yard when I heard the gunshot. So I grabbed the two little ones and began running them into the house. I thought DeRonn was coming in behind us, but I did not see him anymore that night. A lot of police showed up shortly after and started roping off the back yard."

"Did they ever interview you or tell you what was going on?" the Defense attorney asks.

"No."

"So it is your testimony that Mr. DeRonn Johnson was with you in the moments just prior to when the fatal shot was fired?"

"Yes."

"I have no more questions at this time Your Honor."

"State, your witness" the judge directs.

"No questions Your Honor" the Prosecution informs.

"Then you may step down Mr. Catchings. Defense, you may call your next witness," the judge directs.

"The defense rests at this time."

DeRonn Johnson, still smiling arrogantly leans over to his team of Defense lawyers and begins to chat. After a few moments, he sits back into the chair and confidently awaits the closing remarks from his Defense team.

The Defense attorney calmly paces the length of the jury box addressing the holes in the States Case against DeRonn Johnson. The Defense then asks the jury to place themselves in Mr. Johnson's shoes, pointing out the reason his prints were on the gun, and the reason he ran from the police that night. The Defense attorney asks each juror to put themselves in his client's shoes, and what would they do if two men ran at any of them with guns yelling "Get Him." What would they do if several unknown men kicked in their front door to their house? Lastly, the Defense pointed out that Mr. Catchings was with Mr. Johnson at the time the homicide occurred across the alley in the back yard.

As the closing remarks are concluded, the judge gives the jury instructions and orders the jurors to come back with a decision for each of the charges.

After several hours of deliberation, the jurors, Defense attorneys, Prosecuting attorneys, and court staff are held in recess until the following morning. The jurors re-adjourned and deliberated for several more days before finally reaching a decision.

The judge calls the court to order and asks, "Has the jury reached a verdict?"

CHAPTER EIGHT: The Way The Cookie Crumbles

"...That's The Way The Cookie Crumbles..."

With news of the pending verdicts about to be read, the already packed courtroom seems to be bursting at the seams as even more officers, news media, family and friends of both the accused and the victims, all try to squeeze their way into the room. There was a low murmur of voices that quickly escalated to a constant chatter amongst the courtroom. Tension is thick. The Prosecuting attorneys and Defense attorneys anxiously await the reading of the verdict in this high profile case. The defendant, DeRonn Johnson sits next to his lawyers with what seems to be a relaxed calm. A smirk is on his face as he looks back at the standing room only courtroom crowd.

BANG, BANG, BANG...."ORDER. ORDER IN THIS COURTROOM!" the Judge yells as he hammers the gavel.

"Has the jury reached a verdict?" he asks.

"Yes, Your Honor, we have," answers the jury foreman.

"Will the Defendant please rise?" asks the judge.

As DeRonn Johnson rises to his feet, the rooms chattering voices all become silent. No one moves. No one is talking. The silence becomes deafening as all attention is directed toward the jury box and the jury foreman.

"As for count one, Murder in the first degree of Officer Xavier, we the jury find the defendant, DeRonn Johnson,... NOT GUILTY."

There was a brief pause as the courtroom listens in stunned silence.

"As for count two, Attempted Murder of Officer Young, we the jury find the defendant, DeRonn Johnson, ...NOT GUILTY."

By now, there are numerous outbursts being made by the hundreds of fellow officers and their families. The media is scrambling to cover the breaking news, outbursts become uncontrollable, and DeRonn Johnson continues to taunt the officers with his arrogant demeanor and smirks.

"ORDER. ORDER...ORDER IN THIS COURTROOM!" the Judge yells, all the while banging the gavel like a carpenter's hammer to a nail.

Several minutes pass before the Jury Foreman may continue with the reading of the verdicts. Several people have to be forcibly removed from the courtroom after more outbursts are heard.

After several more minutes, the Jury Foreman is instructed to continue.

"As for count three, Attempted Murder of Officer Robinson, we the jury find the defendant, DeRonn Johnson, ...NOT GUILTY."

"As for count four, Obstructing an Official Investigation, we the jury find the defendant, DeRonn Johnson,....GUILTY."

"As for count five, Unlawful Possession of a Firearm, we the jury find the defendant, DeRonn Johnson, ...NOT GUILTY."

At this point, the crowded courtroom is overcome with outbursts. No one can hear the banging of the gavel, or the yelling of the judge. Numerous shoving matches break out between the officers and the family members of DeRonn Johnson. The team of Defense lawyers are seen celebrating their victory with DeRonn Johnson and his family. The Prosecuting attorneys are demanding an immediate appeal. There is a sense of catastrophic loss and dismay amongst the officers and the prosecutors. The media newscasters and reporters are immediately beginning to broadcast the results nationwide as this killer has been acquitted. After another several minutes pass, the Judge regains order in his courtroom. Dismayed at the verdicts reached by the jury, he begins to speak.

"Mr. Johnson, you have tried by a jury of twelve of your peers. You have been acquitted of all felony charges. However, you have been found guilty of the lesser charge, Obstructing an Official Investigation. This charge carries a maximum penalty of one year's confinement in a state penitentiary. The court takes into account the fourteen months you have spent confined to a cell awaiting trial, and considers that as time served. You are free to go. Ladies and Gentlemen of the jury, this court would like to thank you for your services. This court is dismissed."

An elated and relieved DeRonn Johnson is escorted out the courtroom by his team of lawyers. As he passes Officers Young and Robinson, he smirks. The officers both make eye contact with DeRonn Johnson as he comments, "That's the way the cookie crumbles." With that statement, DeRonn Johnson is escorted away from the riled up, and angry group of officers.

Later that evening, Officer Young is in his bedroom getting dressed for work. His wife and child sit on the bed watching TV. Just as Officer Young leaves the house for work, the local news reporter begins to talk.

"Up next in the news, NOT GUILTY! That's the verdict tonight for a man charged with Murder and several counts of Attempted Murder of Police Officers on Chicago's West side. But first, a breaking story. The bodies of an older couple were found today in the trunk of a car on Chicago's West side. Both had been shot in the back of the head. The bodies were identified as Mr. Theodore Catchings and Mrs. Diane Catchings. Police are investigating and have no one in custody at this time."

As Officer Young arrives at work and makes his way to the locker room, the usual voices can be heard as officers talk and joke around while checking their equipment before Roll Call. As Roll Call begins, the Command Lieutenant does the usual inspection of his troops and their equipment before addressing the districts problems of the day.

"As many of you already know, DeRonn Johnson is back on the street. The justice system let us down, and allowed this thug, this killer, to once again walk the streets. Now this I take personally. Many officers risked their lives, and one gave his life, for the capture of this man. And now, he's back out? That's a crock of bull! If you come across this man, and he so much as J-walks, I want him in here. Now, over by Kostner and Roosevelt they found two bodies executed in the trunk of a car. Several units are already over there. The bodies have been identified as Mr. And Mrs. Catchings. We don't have a motive at this time. Be safe ladies and gentlemen. Dismissed."

"Catchings, huh?" Cliff states to James.

"How ironic. The trial ended today, and DeRonn's only witness for his defense is also named Catchings."

"Could be coincidence, doubt it, but it could be."

"Well, let's get outta' here" James adds.

"Cliff, James, radios! They are calling you over the radio," Officer Barnes informs.

"Thanks. Man, we haven't even left the station good and they are already hitting us on the radio. 'Westside 14, are you calling us?" James answers.

"Westside 14, yes. There is a call of a suspicious car circling the block at Douglas and St. Louis, but no description of the car," the dispatcher informs.

"Westside 14, we copy. En-route."

Minutes later, the two officers are at the intersection of Douglas and St. Louis parked and observing the vehicle traffic.

"All these cars seem to be either going or coming, none circling the block," Cliff says.

"Yeah, we'll come clear from this. 'Westside 14, no suspicious car seen. Put us clear," James informs the dispatcher.

"Westside 14," the dispatcher again calls out.

"Westside 14," James answers back.

"Westside 14, we just got a call from a neighbor saying they heard numerous gunshots coming from inside the next door neighbors apartment on the second floor. The address is 1723 S. Central Park. Do you copy?"

"Westside 14, we copy. En-route."

The two officers then race to the scene with lights and sirens. Within seconds, the two veteran officers are on-scene making their approach to the second floor with guns drawn, looking for a suspect or victim. As they reach the second floor landing, the officers hear a loud thud. Cautiously, the two officers inch closer to the door. Quietly they listen for more noises coming from inside the apartment.

"You hear that?" Cliff asks his partner.

"Yeah, sounds like something being dragged," James whispers back.

Suddenly, the door opens. The two veteran officers immediately take cover and train their eyes and weapons on the open door. They see a hand. Then, another hand, blood-soaked and grasping at the floor. Next, they see the body of a man laying face down, gasping for air. The two officers carefully approach the man, and looking into the apartment notice the rear door wide open.

The man, seeing the police, reaches out, and then utters the words "Michael Catchings."

The man then reaches out again, and turns over onto his back. Officers Young and Robinson immediately notice several gunshot wounds to the man's chest and stomach.

"Michael Catchings did it…Help me," the man restates as he begins to choke on his own blood.

"Yeah. Well, that's the way the cookie crumbles!" the officer stated as DeRonn Johnson took his last breath.

Officially, the detectives never knew who shot DeRonn Johnson that fateful evening. But, the word on the street, is that DeRonn Johnson had the elderly parents of Michael Catchings kidnapped, and held, until Michael would testify and give an alibi for DeRonn. No one was ever charged.

ABOUT THE AUTHOR

C. M. Russell was born and raised in Chicago, IL. After graduating from the University of Illinois/Chicago Campus, C.M. Russell began his career with the Chicago Police Dept. C.M. Russell has drawn upon numerous real-life experiences from this urban city to depict the situations officers face on a daily basis. This, his first book, takes the reader on a virtual ride-a-long with the officers. His account is action packed, suspenseful, and keeps the adrenaline pumping right to the very end.

Printed in the United States
66970LVS00001B/216